BÊTE NOIRE

FEAR IS JUST A POINT OF VIEW

Editors:

A. W. Gifford
Jennifer L. Gifford

P.O. Box 811
Ortonville, MI 48462

www.betenoiremagazine.com

Bête Noire is published by Dark Opus Press a division of Charm Noir Omnimedia P.O Box 811, Ortonville, MI 48062

ISBN-13: 978-0692522745
ISBN-10: 0692522743

Bête Noire Magazine © 2015 Charm Noir Omnimedia

Cover art © 2015 A. W. Gifford

All stories, poems, artwork and photos © 2015 of their respective creators

"The Four Seasons of My Garden" by Bob Johnston, first appeared in *Pasque Petals* Fall, 2012

"Masks" by Dan J. Fiore, first appeared in Writer's Digest's Competition Collection, Fall 2013

"The Silk that Binds You" by Kelda Crich, first appeared in *Vignettes from the End of the World*, 2014

"Corn-Fed Baby and Gravy" by Christian Riley, first appeared in *Black Treacle Magazine*, August 2013.

In This Issue

CORN-FED BABY AND GRAVY

Christian Riley

The McClemen's residence looked like an abscessed tooth jutting out of the earth, three stories high, flaccid and diseased. It was surrounded by a sea of corn—fields of green presently bending lightly to a southwesterly wind. There was an aged sycamore at the end of the driveway chained to a dog and a goat, and Lawrence Shoemaker at last rolled his Cadillac to a stop in the tree's accompanying shade.

The stink of shit and animal parlayed with a cloud of dust, rising up and through the opened windows of the Cadillac. Lawrence cursed, reached for a handkerchief and covered his nose. When the dust settled, he grabbed his clipboard and stepped outside, shielding his eyes against the rays of a setting sun.

Crossing the driveway to the front porch, Lawrence deftly navigated through piles of dog crap, and more curiously, dozens of cornhusks lying about. Adding to this oddity, he noticed a particular husk hanging cockeyed from an above windowsill. *Hillbillies*, he thought.

The porch groaned like a bitch in heat as Lawrence pressed his weight onto it. One more step forward, and he swore he'd break through. No need to knock with all this ruckus, but he rapped his knuckles on the door anyhow. He absently flipped pages on his clipboard while he waited. He didn't read anything, didn't even recognize what he was staring at for that matter, his mind deep in thought over Happy Hour at the topless bar in town. Last stop, not long now. Lawrence licked his lips, adjusted his crotch; someone was opening the door.

He was greeted with the sweet smell of cornbread, and the fox-like eyes of Delaroy McClemens.

"Yessir...what can I do you for?" asked Delaroy, his voice deep as a well.

"Delaroy McClemens?"

"That's me."

"My name is Lawrence Shoemaker. I'm an investigator for the Office of Fraud and Accountability. Do you have about ten minutes? I need to ask you some questions about your family."

Delaroy scrunched his eyebrows. "Questions about my family?"

"Yes, sir—if you don't mind."

Hesitating, Delaroy glanced over his shoulder, as if inspecting his house.

"Just a few questions, Mr. McClemens."

"Alrigh'. Well come on in, then... I's about to get me some coffee. Would you like some?"

"That'd be nice, thank you."

The two men passed through the front room, and Lawrence noted a few details: a crotchety old woman to his right, wrapped in a blanket—Mama McClemens he guessed—with her eyes fixed two-feet from the television; and a raggedy clad redhead standing on the staircase to his left, eyes fixed on him. The young woman straddled Lawrence's attention like a saddle on a horse, with her wild hair, and perky, bra-less tits, and flimsy tank top cut high above the navel.

"Put some clothes on, Sissy!" barked Delaroy. "Can't you see we got us some company?"

Lawrence almost mentioned that he didn't mind, but quickly thought otherwise. He bit his tongue and followed Delaroy into the kitchen.

"Some questions, eh?" said Delaroy, motioning to a table. "Go ahead and take a seat then."

Lawrence pulled a chair and sat, then rifled through the pages of his clipboard. "Says here that you've got six children, Mr. McClemens."

"Delaroy," replied the old man, setting two cups on the table. "Call me Delaroy." He filled the cups with coffee then sat across from Lawrence.

"Sure thing, Delaroy. As I was saying, I've got some questions about, well, just one of your kids, actually," Lawrence glanced at the clipboard. "Arlow McClemens?"

Delaroy's eyes narrowed with suspicion as he slowly lifted his cup to his lips.

"That wouldn't be the young woman out there, now would it?" continued Lawrence.

"Ah, hell no."

"Hmm," replied Lawrence, flipping a page. "Oh, yes, I see. You've got a daughter named Dacey McClemens."

"That's Sissy. And Arlow McClemens is my youngest boy. Although we just call him Baby."

"Baby?"

"Yep. Baby."

Lawrence shifted in his seat. "Well, you see here, Mr Mc—ah, Delaroy—according to my records, *Baby* should be about twenty-four years old now."

Delaroy flicked a crumb off the table.

"Does that sound about right to you? That Baby is around twenty-four, or so?"

"Yeah, that sounds about right. I s'pose. What'd you say you do again, mister?"

Dacey McClemens slinked into the kitchen just then, her long naked legs waltzing across the room, ass peeking out from denim shorts, firm as a Georgia peach. She made her way to the fridge, then the stove.

Lawrence bit his lip this time then adjusted his crotch from under the table. "I investigate Fraud for the state, Delaroy. And if Baby McClemens is twenty-four years old, then we've got us an issue."

Delaroy cackled like a hyena. "Fraud? Baby? Shit, mister, that boy can't wipe his own ass without getting into a terrible fix. How the hell's he gonna steal anything?"

"Well, actually, apparently he already has. Or somebody representing him, for that matter. He does live here, doesn't he?"

Presently, Dacey was shucking corn at the sink, but then she paused and turned a shoulder. "You saying that somebody stole from Baby?"

"Hush, Sissy!" cried Delaroy. "And didn't I say to put some clothes on?"

Dacey turned back to the sink. "Should I fix a little extra?"

"No thanks, mam," replied Lawrence, raising a hand. "Don't trouble yourself on my account."

"Oh, it ain't no trouble," said Dacey. "All's we're having is corn, and we've got plenty of it, as you can see."

Lawrence made a face—*corn for dinner?*—then coughed. "Ah...that's okay. I don't think I'll be staying long."

"Suit yourself," shrugged Dacey.

Lawrence turned his attention back to Delaroy. "Now, getting back to your son; it seems that he's been collecting general relief from the state for, well, his whole life."

Delaroy blinked. "General relief? What's that?"

"Welfare, Delaroy. Your son's been collecting welfare from the state. And that's why I'm here." Lawrence paused then leaned forward.

"Look, Mr. McClemens; the state policy — with the economy being as it is and all — allows for recipients to receive general relief for a maximum of three years." He sat back, sipping coffee. "Unless of course, there's good reason otherwise — disabled, or what have you. According to our records, your son has been claiming such disability. But there's no proof, and there never has been — and that's what I call a crack in the system." Lawrence smiled then stole a glance at the crack between Dacey's legs.

Suddenly, three loud "thumps" rattled down the walls, coming somewhere from upstairs.

Lawrence looked around, curious. "What was that?"

Dacey peeked over her shoulder.

"Best get that cornbread cooking, Sissy," Delaroy muttered gravely.

Dacey sighed. "Yeah, yeah, I know."

"So, let me get this straight, Mr. Shoemaker," the old man continued. "You're telling me that Baby now needs a reason for getting his checks in the mail?"

His checks, Lawrence sneered silently. "I'm saying, that unless your son is incapacitated in some way, unless he is unable to work a job like the rest of us, then no, he ain't gonna be getting any more of *his checks.*"

"I see," replied Delaroy, rolling his fingers on the table.

Now, the entire house jolted three times, as if a giant were pounding on the roof with an oak tree.

Lawrence sat up with a start. "What the hell *is* that?"

Delaroy leaned back into his chair. "Mister...that's Baby. And yes, he does live here. And he'll be madder than a rattled hornet if he don't get his dinner soon — so get a moving, Sissy!"

Lawrence chuckled nervously. "Beg your pardon?"

"Oh, yeah, Baby's got him a fierce appetite." Delaroy stared proudly at the ceiling. "And that boy takes to corn like his own ma's teats. Cornbread, corn stew. Fritters and grits. Corn pies with goat cheese. Or just plain ol' *corn*, right off the stalk — boy loves his corn." The old man's eyes narrowed once more, predator-like, much to Lawrence's unease. "But then again, if we add a little gravy...Baby'll eat damn near anything."

Lawrence coughed into his elbow. "Okay, then. Well, ah, back to this business of your son and his checks."

"Mister Shoemaker," Delaroy interrupted, "I think maybe you just need to meet Baby."

Dacey dropped an iron skillet on the floor. "Sorry! Jumped right out of my hands, it did." She bent over, giving Lawrence a bird's eye view down her shirt.

"Yeah, let's ah," replied Lawrence, eyes fixed on Dacey's nipples. "Let's meet your son, shall we?"

With a glare, the old man stood. "Well, come on then."

Delaroy lead Lawrence back through the front room, and up the stairs. There was a sour odor lingering on the third floor, thick and rank as bad cheese, and Lawrence was noticeably bothered, as he covered his nose with his hand. A dark hallway stretched further into the gullet of the house, where light oozed through the cracks of closed doors. Lawrence rubbed knuckles into his watering eyes, trailing behind the old man. At the end of the hall, they stopped in front of a door, and Delaroy snickered quietly.

"What was that fancy word you said? Incapacitated?" Delaroy pushed the door open and stepped to the side.

Lawrence's first thought was of a beached whale. He dropped his lower jaw and leaned forward, staring. Baby McClemens sat in the middle of the room, encompassing the entirely of it, with his six-foot girth, and eight-foot height. He was naked, save for a yellow bed linen used as a diaper, long since needing changed. The corpulent mass of his belly and flanks were strafed with vertical stretch marks, crisscrossing the countless rolls of blubber circling his body. Rounds of fat at his ankles looked like hundred-dollar cheese wheels. And rivulets of slobber trailed down Baby's chin, chest, and belly, ending in pooled globules on the floor. Topping it all was a hairless head the size of a watermelon, bearing a baby-face if there ever was one.

"Bagabba-goo," cooed Baby, slapping his heavy foot on the floor, rattling the walls. He gave a stretch and a belch and Lawrence spotted gummy smegma seated between the tot's layered skin. Then a raspy spray of spittle exuded from Baby's banana-sized lips, preceding a sudden expulsion of corn-chunked bile, splashing out and onto the monstrosity's great belly.

Lawrence's second thought, as he took a step back, was how many beers it would take to cleanse his palate; the odiferous air being so bad, he could taste it. "Sweet mother of Jesus..." he muttered, swallowing the lump in his throat.

"BOOGABBA!" Baby suddenly roared.

And Lawrence's third thought—his final thought—as he went limp on his way straight to the floor, was *Goddammit, I just might miss Happy Hour this evening.*

"Think I kilt him, Pa?" Dacey hovered over Lawrence's still body, iron skillet in hand. "I's about sick and tired of him staring at me like he was—sick ol' pervert."

The old man rubbed his chin. "Maybe so," he said, pushing a boot into Lawrence's side. "Makes no difference, though." He looked at Baby then: a quivering mass of blubber staring back with anxious eyes. "And you go on and hush, now! We'll get you you're supper, already."

Down the hall and at the top of the stairs, Delaroy leaned over the rail. "Get in the kitchen, Ma!" he shouted, glancing over his shoulder at the body of Lawrence Shoemaker. "Looks like Baby's gonna need some gravy!"

Christian Riley's stories have appeared in over sixty magazines and anthologies. As a previous citizen of the Pacific Northwest, he vows one day to return, knowing that that which has yet to be discovered lurks somewhere behind the Redwood Curtain. He keeps a static blog of his writings at frombehindthebluedoor.wordpress.com, and can be reached at chakalives@gmail.com.

The Four Seasons of My Garden

Bob Johnston

The first leaves droop from the branches,
Dirty green, like last year's nettles.
Faded yellow forsythia blooms
Drop petals to the unforgiving ground.

A dusty sunset glows blood-red,
Reflected on the pavement.
The ground heaves and flows like lava,
Then settles back in waves of vapor.

The last leaf falls from twisted branches,
In fading light; brown gives way to gray.
The sun and moon and stars disappear.
Only the dark remains, encircling darkness.

White silence shrouds the earth
In frozen fog and crenulated air.
Fields, trees, and voiceless words
Rest in troubled peace.

Bob Johnston *is a retired petroleum engineer, translator of Russian literature, and an ex-drunk. He started to write serious poetry at age sixty; and now, more than three decades later, he is still trying to catch up. His poems have appeared in twenty-odd journals and in a collection of his poetry titled* At the Rim *(Sunstone Press, 2011). His poems reflect a dim view of the universe and outrage at having been propelled into a century he will never understand.*

FAMILY PORTRAIT *by Sandy DeLuca*

Sandy DeLuca's *art has been exhibited widely throughout New England. In addition, her artwork has been featured as cover art and interior art for various publications, including notable such as the* Bram Stoker *winner,* **Vampires, Zombies and Wanton Souls,** *for Marge Simon's poetry.*

Sandy has also written and published numerous novels, several poetry and fiction collections, an art chapbook and several novellas. As an author she is known for dark and surreal prose; often visceral and shocking. She is best known for her work in the horror genre. However, she has written noir fiction, fantasy, urban fantasy and mainstream fiction as well.

She was a finalist for the **Bram Stoker Award** *for poetry award in 2001, with* **Burial Plots in Sagittarius;** *accompanied by her cover art and interior illustrations. A copy is maintained in the* **Harris Collection of American Poetry and Plays (Brown University) Poetry, 1976-2000.** *She was nominated once more in 2014, with Marge Simon, for* **Dangerous Dreams.**

MEASUREMENTS

Florence Grey

Twenty one grams.
The weight of my soul.
A single wish.
A saddened tear.
Twenty one grams.
The weight of sorrow.
Of painful regret.
A disenheartened sigh.
Twenty one grams.
The weight of a broken heart.
A soft cry.
Single word of goodbye.

Florence Grey *has been writing poetry for nearly twenty years. She loves the swing and big band era and prefers writing her poetry with pen and paper to that of a computer.*

The Silk That Binds You

Kelda Crich

I emerge from the basement into a city blanketed in thick silk. Morning is the safest time to be above ground. The major webs have been painted, but you never know if a spider has been spinning in the night. In the morning, dew clings to the new webs, the trip wires, the invisible tunnels.

When you have new gods, you must change your songs to praise them. In the temple we weave our praise, crashing cymbals, biscuit and dustbin lids, imitating the sounds of the spiders' clacking mandibles. In this way, we can congregate without being attacked.

When a spider walks into the congregation, we part like the Red Sea. It's a youngling. Its eight delicate legs click along the nave. Silk extrudes from the spinnerets on its banded abdomen.

At the altar it lowers its head to the floor. Then, with a hydraulic hiss and the smell of ozone, it extends it legs until its head brushes the vaulted ceiling. We tremble, although it's extremely rare for a spider to kill in a temple. We think they like the worship.

After the spider leaves, a man runs into the nave and gathers the silk.

I touch his arm. "Leave it, my friend."

"This is holy silk," he says.

I slap his face. "Never say that again," I tell him. "Never believe it." I don't care what horror he's seen. I don't care if he's seen his family trapped in a web, injected with digestive juices, sucked dry. "If you say that again, I'll kill you."

The alien spider silk falls from his fingers and pools to the floor.

This charade of worship we created as an excuse to gather is becoming real. I'll need to address that at the next meeting.

On my way home I cut fungus from the spider silk, food for my new family. I live in the school's basement, with a dozen children. I still teach.

I teach them that life has always been a trap, a web of unseen forces entangling us in expectations, and wrapping us, invisible.

I teach them that with the coming of these spider aliens, we see the threads that restrict us. We can find a way to cut through.

I teach them that the spiders are not gods. I teach them that we are not flies in the web.

I teach them a new song.

Kelda Crich *is a new born entity. She's been lurking in her creator's mind for a few years. Now she's out in the open. Find her in London looking at strange things in medical museums or on her blog:*
http://keldacrichblog.blogspot.co.uk/.

Kelda's work has appeared in the Lovecraft E-zine, Journal of Unlikely Acceptances, The Mad Scientist Journal *and in the* Bram Stoker Award *winning* After Death *anthology.*

Three O'Clock Hunt

Alan G. Phillips, Jr.

Frozen solid beneath me,
My boots hit the ground.
Crisp and cold for the morning,
Two ears trace the sound.
Faintly at first,
Then clear with each step
Is the breath of the stalker;
That night shadow walker
Who just killed off nine, or maybe ten;
Released, free from jail
To do it all over again.
I'm by the remnants of ruin,
But I know what he's doin';
You see, here's where it ends,
As he joins his old friends
In those unholy graves;
My weapon targets
What *their* justice saves.
The hard work is done now;
There is time left for sleep,
As the shepherd goes home
To begin counting his sheep.

Alan G. Phillips, Jr.'s *published poetry includes "Cliff-Hanger's Psalm" in* Falling Star Magazine *(2010) and "Ichabod's Return" in* Midnight Screaming Magazine, vol. 2, no. 3 *(Summer 2010).*

His poem "Vacant Intersections" appeared previously in the online maga-zine Moonlit Path *(2010) and was recently featured in the May 2015 issue of* Bloodbond magazine.

He has also published short horror fiction, "The Phoenix" in Gathering Darkness *(Halloween 1994) and "Marzipan Man" in* Moonletters, *issue #3 (October/November 1995).*

He currently lives in Bloomington, Illinois.

Miss Opal

Dennis Day

The summer of '34 was hot. Not much rain for two years, sun a halo in the sky, dust clouds rolling in from the west. A man in a worn suit choked into a bandana, black snot when he blew his nose, head down against the wind. No money. No food. No work. Sympathy in farmers' eyes when he knocked, but they took one look and asked "What kinda farm work you ever done, son?" None of them had a penny to spend. And their wives were scared of him, all but the one who came to the door and gave him a plate to eat by the pump.

Elms meshed over the street — a cathedral were it not for the parching wind and withered leaves — and fine dust spread in black dunes across the sidewalk. Clapboards were grey and rags poked beneath window sashes.

"Hey there, mister."

He turned toward the voice and squinted.

"You looking for work? I've got chores need doing."

He couldn't see her rightly, just a shape on the porch. Her voice was muffled from the kerchief she held over her mouth.

"Come up here where I can see you," she said. "I don't like yelling at men in the street."

The house was cool and dark. Shadows crept up the sofa over tasseled cushions and trembled against patterned wallpaper.

"My name's Opal." She held out her hand and shook his firmly. "And yours?" Far away the wind shushed softly.

"Ryan. From Indiana. On the road most this year."

"And you're only just now getting here, Mr. Ryan? You must be a slow walker. Take a seat while I prepare tea."

In two corners ferns cascaded over wire stands, a harmonium hoarded most of one wall, a picture of the Last Supper another, the heavy divan and chair, a display cabinet crammed with knick-knacks. He looked down at a pocket watch behind the glass.

"That was my daddy's," she said from behind. "I gave it to him when he left for France. One of his buddies picked it up out of the mud and sent it back."

He looked over his shoulder at her.

"Do you take cream or sugar?" she asked with a smile.

He was aware of the grit in his hair and beard, the patina of dust on his scabbed lips. The cup was fragile and the tea scoured his throat. "Sorry 'bout my clothes, ma'am. I don't mean to dirty up your place."

"That's quite alright, Mr. Ryan. I so seldom use this room. Perhaps I can put you to work cleaning it. That is, unless you consider housework beneath you?"

"Well, ma'am, I'm gonna need a place before dark. Thanks for the tea, but I hafta be on my way in a bit."

"You didn't answer my question," she replied. She held her cup poised halfway to her lips and stared at him. "I asked if you consider housework beneath you?"

"No, ma'am, I don't. It's not what I'm used to. But a fellow can't be choosy."

"And what wages do you ask?"

"Like I was saying, ma'am, I hafta be getting along pretty quick."

"Including board and room. What wages do you ask for your labor?" she insisted.

His focus faded to the saucer in her hand, her slender fingers, and back to her face. "You got anybody living here, ma'am? A boarder maybe?" She did not reply. "Folks in towns like this don't take to a man living under the same roof with a woman he ain't married to." He glanced again at her hand holding the delicate saucer.

"Are you a man of fragile sensibilities, Mr. Ryan?" She stared at him coldly. "As for me, I am not. I do what I please and let my neighbors worry about the rest. I hire whom I wish, when I wish, pay them what I wish and board them if I wish." She took a discreet sip of tea. "And so I'll ask you again, Mr. Ryan—are you a man of fragile sensibilities?"

The room felt cool to his skin and the wind was far away. He thought it over.

"No, ma'am, that I am not."

He offered to sleep in the basement, but she'd have none of it. "Who knows what demons lurk there?" she joked. She put him instead on a cot in the pantry next to the kitchen. "I rise late," she said. "The grinder's in the cupboard by the sink and the beans next to your cot. I like to waken to the aroma of coffee in the air."

The wind blew all that night and she put him to work in the morning with a duster. "This work may be new to you, Mr. Ryan, but you must learn to do it carefully. Take each piece in your hand and gently brush the feathers over it. And do try to put things back where you find them."

He moved around the room at his work, but when he glanced at the dull light through the window, he saw motes, millions of them, churning in the air. "You'll need to do it twice a day just to keep ahead as long as the wind blows," she said. "After that, you can get the sweeper up and give the rugs a brushing."

The noon whistle dovetailed with the wind and she ordered him to sit at the kitchen table. She placed a bologna sandwich, potato salad and a pile of pickles before him, then retired with her own plate to the dining room. When he came for her dishes, he found her gazing out the window, her teacup in her hand.

"I need fresh eggs from the grocers, Mr. Ryan. You can pick up a bag of flour while you're at it." She handed him her cup and saucer. "No use trying to conceal you. The sooner they start talking about it, the sooner they'll get tired of it." She looked up into his eyes. "These are friendly folks around here, Mr. Ryan. If anyone should have the nerve to ask, simply say 'I work for Miss Opal' and leave it at that. Do you understand?"

❧✠☙

Mrs. Graettinger's head barely crested the counter on which he placed eggs, flour and a packet of tobacco and papers. Dust swirled in the street and across the wooden floor whenever the door opened. She looked up from her tally sheet.

"For Miss Opal? You want me to put tobacco on Miss Opal's bill?"

He felt every head turn to look at him, but when he glanced right and left, only an old man in bib overalls and a three-day beard grinned back at him.

"Sure, add it on. By the way, if a fellow was to have a thirst, where'd he get it taken care of round here?"

"The pump," Mrs. Graettinger teased. She grinned up at him. "But that ain't what you had in mind. If it's what you're looking for, take a look behind the furnace. Miss Opal's got modern tastes, don't she, Tyle?"

The old man licked his lips and grinned again.

"Gussie rang this afternoon when you were out."

The kitchen felt like a coal at the center of a fire, all the windows closed against the wind, the oven pulsing in the corner. He sat at the table, a black-backed bible in front of him.

"She asked did I approve the tobacco." She paused stirring the bowl, put one hand on her hip and pointed the wooden spoon at him. "I am not adverse to smoking, Mr. Ryan. But not in this house."

He smiled and fingered the corner of the Holy Writ.

"It won't happen again," she said. "In the future, she'll give you only what I phone ahead. And the tobacco is out of your wages. Do you understand?"

He smiled broadly. "Sure I do, ma'am."

"And stop calling me 'ma'am.' It's 'Miss Opal' to you."

"Yes, ma'am, Miss Opal," he said.

She glared. "2 Samuel 16:1. Top shelf on the right."

"What?" Her words didn't make sense.

"Look it up. You'll not be unfamiliar with Scripture in this house, Mr. Ryan. Go ahead, look it up."

He flipped the pages back and forth and ran his finger down one column.

"I get it," he said. "David's servant had a hundred bunches of raisins." He groaned out of his chair and disappeared into the pantry. He put the crock on the table beside her. "You want a hundred bunches?"

"Just the three-quarters cup will do," she said, her hands still on her hips.

Meekly he scraped the raisins into the measuring cup and placed it next to her mixing bowl.

"Now, Mr. Ryan, Genesis 43:11."

Spiraea drooped alongside the garage. In the gloom it was hard to tell if the sun had set or another dark cloud was rolling in from the west. Gusts rushed round the corner and trees danced stiffly. He leaned against the wall, his back to the wind, carefully spreading tobacco in a V-shaped paper between his fingers. He cupped his hands so closely he felt his palms singe, flipped the match into the air and watched it fly away. The smoke was harsh, made sharper by his dry throat.

The back door of the house led through the pantry into the kitchen and a faint light shone from the parlor beyond. He messed his hair and brushed the sleeves of his shirt, but the dust clung to his arms and his lips were dry.

"Will you have another piece of cake, Mr. Ryan?" she asked moving away from the window through which she had been watching him smoke. "I don't take spirits myself, but I know men often do at bedtime. There is a jar on a shelf in back of the furnace. Don't confuse it with the rat poison."

She flipped the switch and a cone of light spread into the room leaving the corners in shadow. She brought the pan to the table, carefully lifted the lid and reached into the drawer for a long-bladed knife.

He poured a small glass and scraped back his chair.

"I'm not your first man, am I, Miss Opal?"

She slid a slice of cake onto a plate. She didn't offer him a fork and watched him swivel his head for his first large bite.

"No, Mr. Ryan, you are not," she smiled. "People must think I'm soft, but it pains me to see so many men on the road, destitute and out of work."

"How come there's no one here now?"

"Your predecessor left suddenly. I gave him his shoes and he walked out and didn't come back." She gazed at the door over his shoulder.

"You gave him his shoes?"

She smiled demurely. "If you leave your shoes by the parlor, Mr. Ryan, I will clean them and return them to you in the morning."

"Don't bother," he said looking down at his scuffed Oxfords. The brogues over the toes were filled with dirt. "When you got only the one pair, they get to be kinda dear."

"Oh, it's no trouble at all," she said raising her hand as if to brush away his concern. "It reminds me of my daddy when he was alive."

Next morning the wind dropped suddenly. Dawn spread over a monotone landscape, its pink and orange rays absorbed by the dust.

"There must be half the county blown into the driveway," she said over coffee. "I'll find my coveralls and see what I can do with it."

"You don't need to do that dirty work," he said. "I'll take care of it."

"No, Mr. Ryan, you are needed indoors. Perhaps you can finally get the parlor dusted decently, the windows washed and the rugs swept. I can manage the driveway."

She told him to wear an apron although he felt foolish when he saw himself in the mirror. Every few minutes he cracked the front door, shook the feather duster vigorously and returned minutely to each piece in the parlor, every knick-knack she'd collected over the years.

From his back pocket dangled a dampened cloth and towel to wash the window and the glass of the display cabinet. He picked up the old pocket watch, blew on it and wiped it with his cloth. He stared at the inscription on the back. When he was through with all the gimcracks in the case, he picked the watch up again and turned it over. With a frown he put it back on the shelf, closed the door and reached for the Last Supper.

There was no fireplace, just the furnace in the basement, and as November shouldered autumn out of the way, they brought their chairs up close to the stove. It was too cold for a smoke and he cradled his evening ration of booze and leaned towards the dying warmth of the oven. She stared into the empty space as if it were a campfire.

"I told you all there is to know 'bout me, Miss Opal," he said. "But you ain't told me nothing 'bout you. How come you live in this old place all by yourself?

"Because I enjoy it, Mr. Ryan," she said.

"Was it your daddy's before he got killed?" He glanced over at her. "Or do you mind talking about that?"

"No, Mr. Ryan, I do not mind. My daddy and I were very close. We loved each other very much."

"And your momma?"

"My mother was a cold woman, Mr. Ryan. She didn't understand what daddy was facing and was no comfort to him."

"But you was close to him? Is that why you give him that watch before he shipped out? How old musta you been? Fourteen? Maybe fifteen?"

"It was a reminder for him of the time when we would be together again. But the war took him from me."

"Your mother musta been stricken."

She turned on him. There was a blush on her cheek and her eyes were hard. "We never spoke of it. There was no body, no funeral. I dealt with my grief and she with hers. She died and that was all there was to it."

He was silent for a moment, but then plunged ahead. "When I was dusting, I noticed there was an engraving on the back of that watch. It said it was from Emma. Was that your momma?"

Her voice was flat. "She took it from me and had her name put on it. But I told him it was from me. Every time he looked at it, he thought of me." She glared into the oven, the fire that wasn't there. "And that was that. We never spoke about it."

Later he slipped his shoes off and left them by the parlor. He padded into the pantry in stocking feet, carefully stropped his razor for his morning shave and pulled the blanket up under his chin.

Three days later a dump-truck backed up the driveway and a man in a smudged uniform slid a chute through a basement window. They stood together watching the coal pile up along the wall of a little room next to the furnace. A dust like summer settled around them.

She slid a long metal table away from the furnace. There was a smear of blood along one edge. "When they aren't scrawny," she explained, "I buy a hen from Tyle for Sunday dinner. He's probably devoured all the brood himself by now."

She grasped a handle sticking from the grate in both hands and shook it violently. "There's the bucket," she said.

He opened the grate and bent and shoveled ashes and clinkers into the pail. "Where you want me to put it?" he asked.

"You can spread it on the drive each morning. But save back a bucket in case we get ice."

She opened the flue and kindled a pile of sticks, waited until it was a bed of embers and then spread one layer and then a second and a third of coal, waiting until each ignited. Then she piled on as much fuel as would fit through the door until the blue flames flickered and bounced shadows off the stone walls.

She turned to him. "There. That's taken care of. I will bank the fire each evening before I go to bed, but you must come down in the morning, clean out the ashes, fill the shuttle and stoke the fire. Do you understand?"

With heat rising from the registers, the house began to feel cozy. He tended the furnace and each day moved from room to room repeating his chores, and then repeated them again and again. When there was no wind, he stood under the eave at the corner of the garage stomping his feet and breathing out steam and smoke and she watched him through the window by the sink.

After he finished the supper dishes each evening, she placed the bible beside him on the kitchen table open to a passage. When she retired to the parlor, he read the newspaper. He slipped his shoes off each night and each morning they were outside the pantry, clean and polished.

He heard squawking one morning in the kitchen. She stood by the sink with a hen hugged firmly beneath one arm while she fished in a drawer with the other and took out a cleaver.

"Boil the water and follow me to the basement with the pail."

He set the pot on the stove and filled the pail. A wave rebounded from one side and sloshed over the side onto his shoes and the dirt floor. She glanced at him disapprovingly and pointed at a log standing on end next to the wall. She stroked the bird with a feather until it calmed, laid its neck gently on the block and took its head with a single blow. She held it by its legs, wings flapping madly, while it bled out into the drain. While it still twitched, she plunged it into the pail.

"Have you ever plucked a bird?" she asked. "Come here and I will show you."

She quickly wound a length of wire around the legs and hung the carcass from an overhead pipe.

"Here, let me guide your hand," she said. Her fingers were cool on top of his. "Don't take too many at a time and pull gently. The fewer the pin feathers, the less work for later."

She took handfuls of feathers from him and tossed them through the grate into the furnace. An acrid smell filled the room. She placed the chicken on the metal table and quickly eviscerated it. She dipped it once again in the pail and handed the body to him.

"Take that upstairs and start in on the pins. I'll clean up down here."

The bird was scrawny and its skin slipped back and forth as he tried to grasp the tiny feathers. He didn't hear her come up behind him with the cleaver.

She quickly separated the chicken into pieces for the pan.

Thanksgiving—in the evening after a supper of fried chicken and mashed potatoes and gravy and canned beans on the side, she suddenly shed her sweater and threw it on the chair in the corner. He looked up and stared at her.

"My, it's so warm in here. I don't need that old thing to keep me warm."

She wore a sheer blouse unbuttoned at the top. It draped over the camisole beneath hiding her small breasts. There was a splotch of red on each cheek and she shook her head as she ran her fingers through her hair. She sat back in her chair, folded her hands in her lap and gazed at him.

"Can I get you anything?" she asked with a raised brow.

He watched her under hooded brows.

"I will join you in your libation this evening," she said. "Just a small sip. Heavens know what might come of me if I had more."

She allowed him to serve her. He poured two glasses and placed one on the table before her.

"Here's to you, Opal," he said smiling down at her.

"Why, Mr. Ryan," she said. "You've called me by my Christian name."

◌⊰✠⊱◌

In the morning, the blanket was on the floor beside her bed and the room was stifling. He stretched his hand over the register and felt a blast of hot air rising. He pulled on his pants and found his shoes at the foot of her bed.

She was in the basement standing in front of the furnace, watching the blue flames dance behind the grate. She wore a heavy sweater and hugged herself as if bothered by a chilly wind.

"You okay, Opal?" he asked. "It's damn hot in here. You ain't cold, are you?"

"Don't call me that," she hissed. "It's 'Miss Opal' to you." She turned on him. "And pull that table back over here where it belongs."

She turned and walked up the steps to the kitchen. She paused and called over her shoulder: "Bring up the poison, Mr. Ryan. There's droppings in the garage."

◌⊰✠⊱◌

Static floated from the radio over the aisles of afternoon shoppers.

"Will you be attending services tonight, Miss Opal?" Mrs. Graettinger asked. "Pastor Williams said he'll preach on being a helping hand in hard times."

Miss Opal placed a pound of brown sugar, a packet of almonds and a quart of buttermilk on the counter next to the cash register and Mrs. Graettinger added them to her list.

"That'll be fifty-four cents," she said.

Miss Opal laid a dollar bill on the counter.

"Sorry, Tyle ain't here to carry your sack for you. He's helping set up at the church."

"It's quite alright, Gussie," Miss Opal said. "I can manage."

Mrs. Graettinger fished a paper bag from beneath the counter and began filling it. "What ever happened to that fellow that was living with you?" she asked. "I was getting used to his face. Not a bad-looking sort."

"They're all the same, Gussie. A few weeks in one place and the wanderlust takes them and they're out the door."

"You certainly have a hard time keeping a man in the house, Miss Opal." Mrs. Graettinger looked up quickly, embarrassed at letting her thought slip. "But I imagine they're all the same — a tramp's a tramp."

"Yes, I'm fortunate he didn't carry off half of what I own."

"Did you report him?"

"No, no police were necessary. I found him with my daddy's watch one day and after that I had my eye on him all the time."

Mrs. Graettinger glanced up at her. "Well, good riddance, I say," she said cheerily.

Miss Opal paused and looked out the window at the first few flakes falling from the darkness. "We'll have a white Christmas yet, Gussie — a warm fire in the furnace and tea in the parlor. It's so cozy."

In the street, a thin man with a growth of beard pulled the lapels of his jacket up around his ears.

Miss Opal stopped and looked at him.

"Excuse me," she said. "You looking for work? I've got a few chores need doing."

That evening after church, Miss Opal got down on her knees and crawled into the little space under the eaves next to her bed. There was a row of men's shoes. They were dusty from the summer. Eleven pairs — work boots and scuffed up Sunday-bests worn down to holes in the soles. She placed the oxfords at the end of the row and carefully dusted the rest with her kerchief.

Dennis Day, *happily retired, lives in Wisconsin with his wife. When he's not poking around libraries and courthouses looking for family history, he enjoys writing about people of his parents' and grandparents' generation — those who lived through and survived the Great War and the Great Depression.*

THE CLAN

Marge Simon

This heritage is of the Blood,
by no social credo or relation.
Our passage intense and sensual,
we've become members of a Family
no longer part of that protoplasmic day-mare
that is defined as life.

My sisters call me James,
first born of a noble Irishman,
till Cromwell took us down.
Five centuries have come and gone
and still I feel the pain.

Another hundred years,
& sweet Aimee, a casket girl,
made passage to the Colonies
to settle in New Orleans,
become a respectable mistress
& in Aimee's way, she surely did --
two marks for every neck.

Lisle took off for the Libyan Desert,
hoping to sample Rommel's blood in '41.
Sometimes we see her face
depicted outside bars in Cairo
where various pleasures
may be procured.

Miriam left for Bangladesh in '63,
She was the religious one,
though meditation didn't work.
Still, she likes that filthy place,
perhaps for its music, but more likely
for the ease of gaining veins.

Ling is the oldest of us all,
certainly the most talented as well,
pens songs for rock stars, assists
in their success or failure
depending on her inscrutable mood.

So my sisters come and go –
in the changing face of years.
Though the wine is better
so we're told, it holds no interest.
Manhattan's neon lights
form irreal colors, indistinct
as our own undead lives.

New Years Eve we gather
to watch them from my flat,
dots moving on horizons,
framed in yesteryears,
where tomorrow is a grave
we have yet to leave.

Marge Simon's *works appear in publications such as* Strange Horizons, Niteblade, DailySF Magazine, Pedestal Magazine, Dreams & Night-mares. *She edits a column for the HWA Newsletter and serves as Chair of the Board of Trustees. She has won the Strange Horizons Readers Choice Award, the Bram Stoker Award™(2008, 2012, 2013), the Rhysling Award and the Dwarf Stars Award. Collections:* Like Birds in the Rain, Unearthly Delights, The Mad Hattery, Vampires, Zombies & Wanton Souls, *and* Dangerous Dreams. Member HWA, SFWA, SFPA. *www.margesimon.com*

Mammom and the Two Farmers

Joshua Hampel

The drought made the days seem twice as long as usual, which gave Harry plenty of time after dinner to sit in the barn and stare at the tractor and mentally curse his borrowing money from the bank to buy the new invention and then use it to plow and plant his fields just in time for no rain to arrive.

A field of dying money, that's all he had now.

He was thankful at least that things couldn't get much worse.

"Late hour to be social-like." Harry, thankful for the interruption, looked to his son and went and stood beside him.

Harry and his son Eli watched as their neighbor, Allen Ambry, made his way up the road towards Harry Carlson's farm; his steps leaving low hanging clouds of dust in the still air behind him. The fading sunlight made Allen a moving stain amid the ash grey blanket of dirt that covered the world. "It'll be near dark by time he even gets here," Eli said. "What man leaves his family all alone at night? Reckon it must be somethin right-important?"

Harry looked at his son, taking in his stance that said there wasn't a thing in the world that he was afraid of. "Go inside and help your ma with your sisters." Eli looked at his father before walking out of the barn and across the yard to the front steps of the house. Harry watched him go, and though he wasn't one to pat himself on the back, he was proud of his son and thought he and his wife had done pretty well raising the boy.

"God damned weather, huh," Was the first thing Allen said when he stood before Harry, and after saying it, he laughed. Harry looked at the man before him, taking in the change from smiling and laughing to wincing and sobbing.

"Something happened," Allen started—then seemed to change his mind. "I met someone…he made my hands do things, he took my hands and then at the end gave them back to me just long enough to hold my family before they died." He looked to Harry. "He made me say things, horrible things to them, and then when he let me hold them he let me talk and say that I was sorry, and I didn't know what was going on, and that I was scared.

"I tried to kill myself but he wouldn't let me. He made me get up and walk here instead. He knows he doesn't have to make me say things, or do things, because he promises when I'm done doin' what he tells me he'll let me die, so I do what he wants.

"He's watching though, don't think he ain't.

"He says this whole country is cursed, but you can save it. You, Harry, you can save this country, this drought, all the people and families that will die from what will come. You can save them." Allen pulled a revolver out of his left hip overall pocket, and a dollar bill out of the right one. "Sell him your farm for one dollar. You're family leaves right now, I don't care where you go or what you do, but you have to leave now."

Harry looked at the money and then to his neighbor. "Or?"

"I'll kill your two girls." He wept then, his whole body shaking. "I'm sorry Harry, I really am."

Harry punched Allen as hard as he could, and while Allen stumbled back from the blow Harry grabbed his arm and wrestled the gun out of his hand. Allen stood there, his free hand against his face. "Now get back home, Allen," Harry said. "I don't know what's got into you but if you don't head home now I'll shoot you!"

Allen laughed, or sobbed, or both and said, "The gun wasn't for me, Harry. I don't need a gun to kill your girls. He'd never let me use it anyway, too quick. The gun's for you. You chose the gun over the money so that's that." Allen turned and started to walk towards the house. "I have to do what I have to do, and so do you."

Harry raised the gun. "Allen, keep away from my home, you hear me?"

"I hear you, do you hear me? We're cursed, Harry, you and me. I realized it after what I'd done. Either you realize it now, or after you've lost your twin girls, it's up to you."

"Damn you, Allen!"

Allen nodded as he put a foot on the front step of the house and Harry shot him once in the back. Allen fell to his knees, and stayed there for a second before falling back onto the ground.

Harry lowered the gun and went to Allen and looking down he found his neighbor looking up at him, smiling. "Thank you," he said.

Harry looked away. He looked down to his boots and his eyes picked up the slightest bit of movement from the dust that covered the ground. He felt something behind him, faint movement, and when he turned he saw in the distance a cloud darker than the night, and it was growing.

The wind was picking up already and Harry fought to give any credit to the voice deep in his mind that was telling him he made a mistake.

Joshua Hampel *lives and works in Wichita, Kansas.*

RESUMING STARLIGHT

Herb Kauderer

dark candy clouds scurry across lights of night sky
sickening the cast of moon & planets, & aircraft
sickening even the pricking of starlight that pokes
surfaces of cities & fields & lakes

and beneath such audience asphalt quits tires
& mud lunges to embrace steel & vinyl & chrome
and the love/fear struggle quickly stirs mud so deep
the smell of long decayed meat & newly uncovered dung

sweeps passengers pulling them down
as surely as the mud pulls inorganics home
and in the aftermath all that remains are the odors
of another time & empty tire tracks that call the
cleansing rain that heals memory's scars
& the assault of resuming starlight

Herb Kauderer *is an associate professor of English at Hilbert College and has an MFA from Goddard College. His poetry has recently appeared in* Asimov's, Grievous Angel, Eye to the Telescope, *and many more markets both genre and literary.*

CEMETARY RAVEN *by Midas*

A twenty-seven year old photographer going by his nickname of **Midas,** *opened a studio in 1995 with a goal, to establish a presence in a tiny town where no studios existed. He envisioned a place where up and coming models could develop their portfolios without driving two hours to the nearest city. And to see these models published in print either in ads or articles However in small towns, the talent was scarce and most clients were content with staying home. After a few years without getting a model established and published and with pressure from his fiancé;* **Midas** *closed the doors, sold his cameras and studio equipment and rode west to Tennessee with his soon to be wife.*

Still the idea left behind in small town Virginia never left **Midas.** *Now married and with a child, a subject would catch his eye and could picture the person in a pictorial. However with no camera in his possession, he would never see his visions come to life.*

In 2011, it wasn't much but his family bought him a small point and shoot digital camera and the following year **Midas** *decided to step back into the photography world. And by 2012, social networking opened doors which never existed and he found subjects which became new clients. And by early 2014, he began to work with established models and helped to open doors into publishing.*

Within four months, **Midas'** *work and models have been featured in ten publications. All this with no fancy cameras and no studio just using a camera, flash, and laptop.* **Midas** *is uncertain what will happen in 2015 but he is sure the 27 year old in a small town would be green with envy.*

SEND A FRIEND

Reese LeBlanc

August wanes in the twilight.

In every rambling thicket
roaring insects greet doom with gaiety,
singing in the face of certain death.

The hum breaks on the walls of the farmhouse,
low and stony and secluded.

In here, booze and chatter and unearthed video tapes
form a booming union.

We'll cover every VHS gorefest before daybreak,
while the buzzing woods beyond the softly-lit den
brace for change.

Halfway through the marathon now.

An unwelcome sound disrupts the trilling Southern night,
a faint drumming like digits on wood.

Perhaps there's something out there with the droning bugs,
some oozing freak attempting to make contact.

Perhaps it's a ghostly knuckle rapping on the windowpane.

Perhaps it's a hulking shadow of a thing,
immune to breasts and drugs and love.
Only the skin and brains of the slain satiate,
never denting the masked dumbness
looming in the dark.

Perhaps it's the hillbilly axe people who call these forests
home.

Every year, out-of-towners venture into these woods,
unaware of the threat.

The cretins might be waiting in the gloom this very moment,
their few good teeth poised to grind,
to rend flesh from bone.

Then again,
it might be a moth driven to glass,
a thumping kamikaze paired with the magic of analog.

Send a friend out to look.

Best known for his work as a music critic, **Reese LeBlanc** has contributed to a number of publications. A lifelong student of horror cinema and literature, he hopes to work within the genre with greater frequency in the coming years. .

Masks

Dan J. Fiore

Someone screams.

Jay turns, following his wife's eyes behind him to the front door across the diner.

Three men in wet ski masks and camo hunting gear stand holding guns, their barrels dripping rain. "Phones, wallets, whatever," the man in the orange mask says. "Put all that shit on the table."

Turning back to his wife, Jay raises his hands, fingers spread just above the table, and looks in his wife's eyes. "Syl," he says, his voice a pointed whisper. "Syl."

Her eyes float slowly from the gunmen to her husband. Tears sit locked and quivering between her lashes.

Jay says, "It's gonna be alright." He places a hand over hers. He nods.

Syl blinks and a single tear falls. Removing her hand from under his, she wipes her cheek with her sleeve.

Jay unlatches the watch from his wrist and drops it on the paper place mat in front of him.

Syl, with trembling hands, twists at her finger, removing and setting down between them her silver wedding ring.

Two gunmen—one holding a revolver and the other a hunting rifle—spread through the opposite end of the diner. The gunman in the orange ski mask glances at Jay and Syl as he walks past their table to a family sitting in the corner. With the man's eyes on him, Jay pulls the wallet from his pocket and places it on the table.

Turning to the family's table, the orange-masked man scoops whatever's there into a pillow sack while a young boy sitting in the booth watches him, huddled in his mother's arms.

With the gunman looking down at the little boy, Jay quickly but smoothly grabs up his fork. He slides it under the table, holding it in a tight fist between his knees. Jay notices Syl watching him with her mouth and eyes wide with worry. Before Jay can do anything to calm his wife, the gunman turns away from the boy and heads toward their table.

Syl shrinks in her booth, hunching over.

As the gunman begins gathering their things on the table, his eyes lock on Jay.

Jay stares back, still and calm.

Having taken everything from the table but Syl's wedding ring, the gunman lingers. Jay's ring is still wrapped around one of the five fingers gripping the fork under the table. The two men glare at one another as the man's hold on his pistol pulsates at his hip, his fist like Jay's pounding heart.

The gunman sighs. He clears his throat. Looking down, he shakes his gun and leaves the table.

Jay turns to Syl. She sits frozen, mouth gaping as she watches the gunman walk away. Tear tracks streak down her cheeks. Her shoulders quake.

"Syl," Jay says.

Her eyes once again drift to meet his. They're empty. Hollow.

"Don't worry," he says. "Nothin's gonna happen."

"What do you want?"

"Nothing," she said. "I'm not hungry."

"Order something." Jay handed her a menu.

"I don't want anything."

"Okay." He looked over the menu, eyebrows raised. "Well," he said, "I'm gonna order something."

"Do whatever you want."

Through his teeth, he said, "Don't have to say it like that."

Syl shrugged and Jay followed her eyes out the window to a broken-down Impala across the road.

"Should we start back home?" she asked.

"Why?"

"The rain," she said.

"Didn't see no clouds." He glanced back at her.

"They're behind you, up across town." Nibbling on the ragged cuff of her sweatshirt, Syl looked down at Jay's hands. "We should leave."

"We didn't even order." His eyes dropped to his own scar-crossed knuckles. Leaning back, he set the menu flat on the table and slid his hands to his lap where neither of them could see.

"But the rain..."

"I want pie," he said. He lowered his head and studied the menu. "It's Sunday. It's tradition."

Barely a breath later, she pleaded, "Let's just go."

"I don't even see no clouds," he said without looking up from the menu.

"Please."

The waitress came. "The usual, Jay?" she asked smiling. He nodded and told her what pie he wanted.

She turned to Syl. "And for you, Sylvia?"

"Nothing." She gave a weak smile. "Thanks."

"'Least get a coffee," Jay said. "Somethin'."

"Fine."

"A coffee?" the waitress asked, raising her drawn-on eyebrows.

Syl nodded and stared back out the window.

"The fuck you say?" a voice calls out.

Syl's ice-blue eyes widen.

Jay turns around in his booth. The man in the orange mask stares right at him. He shouts, "You givin' me shit?"

Jay looks around, tightening his fingers around the slick metal between them.

The gunman marches toward him.

Whimpers and gasps spread through the diner as the man raises his gun in Jay's face.

"I didn't say nothin'," Jay says, getting up. "We don't—"

The butt end of the man's pistol sends him sprawling back into his booth. By the time Jay sits up again, the man has Syl on her feet with his arm wrapped around her neck. "Say shit now," the gunman says. "Do something." His barrel's buried in her golden blonde hair. "Come on, man. Fuckin' do something," he says. "Do it."

Jay raises his empty hand as blood rolls down into his beard. "I didn't say nothin'. We don't want no trouble. Just, let her go. Please."

The man turns the gun on Jay. His hand trembles holding it there, aimed right at Jay's bloodied eye.

Syl's unblinking stare locks on Jay. Her chewed-up fingernails dig into the gunman's forearm at her neck, clinging as if she might fall.

For a moment, the room freezes in cold silence, filled only with the rattle of the vent above them and the trickling patter of rain against the roof and windows.

Jay waits, his heartbeat doubling.

The gunman thumbs back the pistol's hammer.

Jay's fingers tighten around the fork held hidden under the table. Then —

A child across the room, the one huddled in his mother's arms, begins to cry.

A long breath escapes the orange-masked man's nostrils. He lowers the pistol and says to no one, "She's coming with us."

Syl blurts out, "What?" And the masked man pulls her toward the exit.

"Wait," Jay says. But the man continues to the front door with Syl shuffling alongside him, her bewildered eyes staring back at Jay over the man's shoulder.

"I hate you," Syl said stirring her coffee.

Jay threw down his fork. Rhubarb flung across the table and onto the sleeve of the bulky sweater Syl sat wrapped in.

A couple looked over from the other side of the diner. Jay forced a smile.

"Stop talkin' like that," he said to his wife.

"What do you want?" she asked.

"To just eat my pie." He picked his fork back up.

"No. What do you *want?*"

He said nothing and instead looked out the window and down the road, following a car as it shrunk toward the flatlands outside town. What once was a raccoon lay heaped, mangled and decaying on the roadside gravel. Jay spooned more rhubarb into his mouth. He looked elsewhere.

The waitress came and, before she could refill their coffees, Jay said, "We're fine," and the waitress walked away.

Tears sat in Syl's eyes. "You're such a stubborn asshole," she said. "Things're gonna end bad for you. All just 'cause you don't know when it's goddamn time to quit."

Still looking out the window, he said, "Your coffee's gettin' cold."

Jay waits until the gunmen walk out the door before getting out of his booth.

As he moves through the diner, he watches them cross the parking lot to their van. A crew of cooks and waitresses stare up at him from under the front counter as he passes.

"Please," the manager says from the kitchen doorway. "Just stay inside, you dumbass!"

With the fork clenched prongs-down in his hand, Jay pushes through the front door and into the rain. The entrance bell chimes, startling Jay into a full-on sprint.

The last gunman stops as the other two keep heading for the van. But by the time he turns to inspect the sound, Jay's already bearing down on him. As the gunman stumbles backward, struggling to pull the revolver from his belt, Jay digs the fork deep into the man's right eye. Blood explodes from behind the mask and the gunman squeals, falling to the rain-puddled ground.

Keeping his momentum, Jay crouches and drives his shoulder into the gut of the orange-masked man while the rifleman hurries Syl into the van from the other side. The hit slams the man in the orange mask's head into the side mirror, sending him heavily to the pavement as Jay's shoulder pops out of place.

Coming around the back bumper, the rifleman fires a shot from his hip. The slug tears through Jay's side, knocking him back. Jay grabs the van's hood to steady himself as he takes long, deep breaths. He doesn't look down at his wound.

Rushing to reload, the rifleman fumbles with the bolt as Jay steadies his footing. He stumbles up to the rifleman, grabs the barrel, and, taking one more deep breath, drives the heel of his boot down into the man's left knee, folding it sideways with a thick, muddy snap. A savage yell erupts from the man's throat as he teeters over. Jay grabs up the rifle and punches the bolt back into place. He staggers, turning around dizzily, and takes aim.

But from the ground the man in the orange mask has his pistol already fixed on Jay.

"Alex!" Syl screams from inside the van. "Don't!"

Jay freezes.

"Please!" she continues, banging on the window. "I changed my mind! PLEASE!"

Lowering the rifle, Jay looks up at Syl. She stares back at him through the rain-glazed window, her face a mess of emotions. He begins to say something. But the gunshot cuts him off.

CRISTO

"I just wish you'd think about it," she said. "I mean, really, really think about it. What are you holding onto here?"

Rain blew against the window, blurring the landscape outside.

"I thought we were done with this," he said.

"We are."

"You know what I mean."

"We can both be done," she said. "We can both be happy."

Jay said, "You don't know that."

Syl said, "You're a coward."

"'Til death do us part, Syl."

"Sure," she said. "Keep that promise."

"Can I just eat my damn pie?"

"I need you to really think about this, Jay," she said, her voice wavering as her eyes narrowed. "Please. Before it's too late."

"Where's all this even comin' from?" He asked her. "What *is* all this?"

"It's nothing." She broke then, saying through sobs, "It's all nothing, Jay. You just don't have the goddamn balls to admit it."

"Then go." He waved a hand. "I ain't giving up. I won't sign no papers. But if all this is nothing to you," he said, "then just leave. Walk out the fuckin' door. Walk home right now, pack up and leave."

"I can't." Syl buried her eyes into the sleeves stretched over her hands. "It's raining. We waited too long."

"So wait longer." Jay looked out at the flatlands in the distance as the front door chimed behind him. "The rain'll stop eventually."

Someone screamed.

CRISTO

Dan J. Fiore *is a freelance writer from Pittsburgh with work published by Writer's Digest, DarkFuse and Thuglit, among others. His short fiction won grand prize in the 82nd annual Writer's Digest Writing Competition and his screenwriting was awarded the Pittsburgh Filmmakers Institute's First Works Grant in 2009. He's currently pursuing his MFA while finishing his first novel. You can follow him on twitter at @danjfiore or find more of his work at* www.danjfiore.com

www.ingramcontent.com/pod-product-compliance
Lightning Source LLC
Chambersburg PA
CBHW071223130626
46555CB00004B/1826